Princess

Princess

by CAROLYN LANE

with illustrations by the author

Cover photo: Creszentia Allen

SCHOLASTIC INC.
NEW YORK · TORONTO · LONDON · AUCKLAND · SYDNEY · TOKYO

For Jay

PRINCESS

ISBN 0-590-30383-X

13 12 11 10 9 8 7 6 5 4 3   3 4 5 6 7/8

Printed in the U.S.A.   28

Contents

Alone

"Princess!... Prin-cess!... Prin-*c-e-s-s!*"

Through the pounding rain, Mary Ellen's high, frantic voice floated over the fields, sounding faint and far away.

Creeping out from under the tangle of thorny bushes that had been her shelter, Princess perked her ears, listening.

"Prin-*c-e-s-s*..."

There it was — just over that way, beyond the pines — there! No — there!

Bewildered, Princess whirled about, meowing forlornly as the lashing rain stung her eyes and soaked into her long white fur. The familiar voice came to her again and again, but the wind blew it this way and that, and she had no idea which way to go.

Plunging into the tall, wet grass, Princess began zigzagging crazily across the fields, trying to follow the tiny sound. But a gust of wind suddenly swept the voice away, and now there was no sound at all but the steady drumming of rain all around her.

Huddled miserably in a clump of dripping weeds, Princess stared into the rainy darkness, searching for lighted windows to guide her home. But it was almost as though the row of beachfront houses had been swallowed up in the storm, and no matter where she looked, there was nothing but a terrifying blackness.

How had she come so far, Princess wondered, just chasing that silly, hopping toad into the fields after supper? Why hadn't she noticed those first gentle drops of rain spattering the ground? And when the downpour suddenly came crashing down on her, why hadn't she dashed for the safety of the back porch instead of diving under a scraggly bush?

She didn't know. All she knew was that Mary Ellen's voice was gone, and that she was alone and wet and lost in the middle of a rainswept field.

Never in all her safe, pampered life had she been so thoroughly wretched. Her long fur, hanging down in sodden clumps, was a mass of sticky burrs, and she knew that her beautiful plumed tail was as limp and wet as the soggy pine needles dripping from the trees.

Shivering with cold, Princess longed for her warm wicker bed under the kitchen stove, for the fluffy towel that would rub her dry, and—yes, even for the stiff wire brush that would get those dreadful burrs out of her fur. She didn't even think she would mind the painful yanking, if she could just be warm and dry again.

But which way was home?

Leaping swiftly to the top of a tree stump, Princess peered once more into the darkness, looking first one way, then another.

There! Just ahead! Suddenly tiny lights were winking at her through the branches of the pines — lights all in a row—and Princess knew she was staring at the back windows of the houses along the beach. One of those lights would be shining from her own kitchen window!

At once, heedless of the brambles that caught in her thick fur, Princess was bounding over the fields toward the familiar back road — and home!

But a blue-white flash of lightning suddenly flamed in the sky, stopping her in the middle of the open field. Terrified, Princess cowered in the grass, looking frantically about for a place to hide.

A mighty crack of thunder jolted the ground under her feet, and then there was another blaze of lightning. And another—and another. The fields all around seemed suddenly aflame, and no matter which way she turned, Princess was dazzled by an eery, glaring whiteness. Through it all the rain kept coming and coming, and the gusting wind nearly blew her off her feet.

Sheltering herself as best she could under a jagged, dripping rock, Princess squinted fearfully out into the storm, starting at every clap of thunder, every flash of lightning. To her surprise, the rain stopped almost as suddenly as it had begun, and soon the last terrible rolls of thunder were fading to a distant rumble.

When the sky was black and silent once more, Princess padded out into the field, listening for the sound of her name in the sudden stillness.

But all she heard was the soft gurgling of running streams, and here and there the chirping of tiny insects in the wet grass. The voice did not come again.

And the lights! Where had they gone, all those lights twinkling from kitchen windows? Dashing first in one direction, then another, Princess explored the misty darkness. But there was nothing—no moon, not even the glimmer of a star—to light the blackness. All she could do was sniff the air, hoping to pick up a scent of the sea or perhaps a whiff of damp, rotting wood that would lead her to the old boardwalk that ran the length of the beach.

But the sticky air smelled of nothing but wet pine needles, and it was still. Until a wind came up, there was no way to sniff her way to the sea.

Curling herself into a tight, damp ball, Princess settled herself under the overhanging rock again. She would try to doze away the long dark night, and when the first light of morning came, she was sure to spot the familiar row of houses along the boardwalk. In no time at all she'd be bounding up the steps of her own back porch.

But morning came, afternoon came—and Princess found herself still wandering hopelessly through strange fields. She saw rows of houses along sandy back roads, but beyond them there was never a glint of the sparkling bay, only more and more fields of waving, drying grass. The brisk little breeze that had sprung up in the night carried no remembered tang of the sea, and Princess knew that home was far away.

Night came once more—dark and frightening and cold—and then another morning. And another, and another. Soon Princess had no idea how long she'd been lost. All she knew was that the circle of light and dark came again and again as she wandered— and with every new day she grew skinnier and uglier.

Sometimes, glancing at her strange reflection in the swampy pools where she drank, it was hard to remember that she'd once been the fluffy, pampered Princess of Avalon who had dined on Tastee Tidbits out of a dish, and slept in a fancy wicker bed with her name on it.

But there were no Tastee Tidbits now—only the little field mice and soggy picnic leavings that barely kept her from starving—and her bed was the cold, hard ground under the scratchy bushes that grew in the fields.

Princess now kept a safe distance from houses— and from people. To her shock and amazement, she was chased furiously away whenever she begged a bit of food and kindness—she, who had been loved and fussed over since she was a tiny kitten! Some people even seemed afraid of her, and once—when she had dared to pad hopefully up the steps of a lighted back porch — an angry man in a bathrobe had actually dumped a bucket of water on her!

Chill, end-of-summer winds were beginning to blow through the fields at night, and Princess knew that soon all the families along the beach would be closing up their houses and heading back to their snug winter homes. Sometimes, dozing fitfully in the damp grass, Princess dreamed that her own house would be closed and silent when she found it, that her family would have gone off without her.

But no! Snapping awake with a shudder, Princess told herself over and over again that the boardwalk was very near now, and that her family would be waiting for her. They'd be out searching the dunes and fields, calling and calling. Soon she'd hear the sound of a familiar voice. Yes, soon!

Longing for morning, Princess would close her eyes again and try to dream of home — not the weathered summer cottage on the boardwalk, but her *real* home back in the city. She always dreaded the long ride in the car, cramped in her stuffy cat case, but this time she thought she wouldn't mind a bit.

Shivering in the dampness, Princess yearned for the cozy hearthrug she had used to curl up on, basking in the golden warmth of the fire...the sunny windowsill where she liked to drowse away her mornings...the good feeling of a brush smoothing her fur...the soft sound of Mary Ellen's voice talking to her...heaping dishes of Tastee Tidbits ...saucers of warm milk...

Her stomach growling, Princess would curl herself into a tighter ball, trying to keep herself asleep so that she wouldn't remember how cold and hungry she was. Soon the bright pictures would begin drifting through her head again, and she could almost feel that she was sleeping on her own plump mattress.

It was on a night when she was dreaming of home that a whiff of something different in the air suddenly brought her wide awake. Springing to her feet, she stood motionless, sniffing the changing wind.

The sea! It smelled of the sea—and it seemed to be coming from just beyond the distant pines. Suddenly she saw tiny lights gleaming through the branches, and beyond them a glint of moonlight sparkling over the bay!

Her nose quivering in excitement as she caught the familiar scent of the salty, splintery old boardwalk, Princess was off at a bound through the moonlit fields.

The Search

The familiar row of houses, suddenly looming at her out of the darkness, seemed far longer than she remembered, and Princess was dismayed to find that she didn't know which of the tall, weathered houses might be hers.

Staring up and down the endless row of front porches, she switched her tail nervously back and forth, wondering what to do. Should she walk the length of the boardwalk, meowing, hoping that Mary Ellen might hear?

No! Suddenly remembering that awful angry man in the bathrobe, Princess decided to hide herself under the boardwalk until daylight. She was in no mood for a drenching!

The sand under the boardwalk was clammy and cold, but Princess didn't really mind. It was, after all, to be her very last night outdoors. Finding an ancient, salt-stiffened old beach towel in a dark corner, she curled herself up on it and closed her eyes. For the first time in all the days she'd been lost, Princess slept soundly all the way into a bright new day.

But it wasn't the glint of sunlight that finally woke her. It was the pounding of small bare feet overhead, sending showers of sand down through the cracks and into her tangled fur. Licking furiously at the stuff, she squinted up through the boards to see if the shower was over, or whether other feet would follow.

They did not. Only a voice followed, a distant child's voice calling out a shrill farewell, and in a moment the footsteps had faded away. Soon there was only the rhythmic breaking of waves on the shore to break the stillness, and overhead the lonely cry of seagulls.

With a hasty, hopeless lick at her fur—now full of sand as well as burrs—Princess crept out into the sunlight and began studying the beach for possible dangers. But she saw only a scattering of children, busily digging holes at the water's edge, and Princess decided they were far enough away not even to spot her. Bravely she scampered up the steps to the boardwalk.

It looked familiar—and yet it didn't look familiar. A strange silence hung over the houses, and Princess was surprised to see a long row of empty porches. Where was everybody? And why, on a beautiful morning like this, were so many windows closed and shuttered? Why were the boats tucked under porches and all covered with canvas? Had they all gone home after all?

But the hum of a vacuum cleaner—and then the distant ring of a telephone—told her that at least a few families were still here. Surely one of them would be hers—and how glad Mary Ellen would be to see her poor lost Princess come bounding up the front steps!

And then, through the screen door of one of the houses, drifted the beautiful, long-forgotten scent of a real breakfast. Bacon! Freshly made toast! Eggs frying in butter! Remembering that she'd had nothing to eat since last night's scrawny little mouse, Princess felt her mouth beginning to water at the mere scent of it.

The good smell seemed to be coming from the house directly in front of her, and at a bound, Princess was crouched at the bottom of the porch steps, excitedly sniffing the air. It wasn't her own house— she knew that from the clump of beach roses blooming in the yard—but maybe the people in it were kind.

Maybe, if she could just clean herself up a bit, they'd see that underneath all those burrs and tangles she was merely a lost housecat, not a dingy, disreputable stray. They'd give her at least a scrap of something then, she was sure of it. And maybe— even though she'd long since lost the little pink collar with her name on it—they'd remember seeing her on her own porch railing, and know where she belonged. They might even take her home!

Frantically, Princess began licking at her matted fur, trying to make herself look like the old, fluffy Princess of Avalon they might remember. But the scratchy, clinging little burrs tore her tongue as she yanked at them, and she knew the task was hopeless. She would simply have to count on her beautiful amber eyes and her tufted ears to tell them who she was.

Just as she was about to scamper softly up the steps, a woman in an apron bumped open the screen door and came out on the porch, carrying a tray. She looked sleepy and cross as she began setting plates and things around the table, and Princess knew enough not to startle her. This was a time for her most elegant manners.

Holding her matted tail proudly aloft, as though it were still the jaunty, well-brushed plume it had been back in the old days, she padded slowly up the porch steps, meowing a pleasant "good morning."

"Oh!" Startled after all, the woman began flapping a napkin at her. "Go away, you mangy old thing! *Scat!*"

"Scat—who? Who're you chasing, Mom?" A little boy came banging through the screen door, and stood staring, wide-eyed, at the frightened Princess. "Hey, that's some fancy cat! Just look at that long hair, Mom, and that bushy tail and everything! It's even got yellow eyes — and regular cats have just plain old green ones, don't they? I'll bet that's a real expensive cat, Mom, and it must be lost. That's why it looks so awful. Gee—maybe we could get a reward if we—"

"Don't you *touch* that creature!" Hastily the lady snatched her boy backwards, a terrified look on her face. "That's a *wild* cat if I ever saw one! People abandon them, and then they go wild. They're dangerous. You never know when they're going to lash out at you. Now you just leave that cat alone! *Scat!*"

"But the poor thing..."

"The 'poor thing' is entirely capable of looking after itself, don't you worry about it. And I will not have you getting yourself scratched, or picking up goodness knows what diseases — *scat!*"

Seizing a broom from a corner of the porch, the boy's mother suddenly began making furious sweeping motions at Princess.

"Go on, now, *get!*"

"Get!" echoed the little boy, frightened now himself. "Scram, you ratty old cat, you! Get off our porch!"

So frightened that she found herself hunching up her back and hissing, Princess whirled and fled, skittering wildly over the boardwalk and down to the sand below. Her heart pounded as she heard the woman angrily thumping the broom handle on the porch steps.

She had never been so shocked in all her life — not even by the man in the bathrobe — and it was not until she had plunged into the safe darkness under the boardwalk that her terror began turning slowly into fury. *Wild* cat, was she? And *mangy?* She, the Princess of Avalon, who had been displayed in the very best cat shows — and even had a blue ribbon to prove it? The little boy had guessed what she was from the start, but that foolish mother of his hadn't so much as glanced at her unusual amber eyes or her tufted ears! Clearly the woman had no taste in cats!

Some day, Princess decided, when she was her old fluffy white self again, she'd parade past this very house and show that snippy lady a thing or two! Just wait till she saw Princess in one of her fancy collars, or maybe the pink ribbon she wore on Sundays. *Then* she'd know what sort of guest she had turned away so rudely. *Then* she'd be sorry!

But it was growing harder and harder now even to think of such things as ribbons and collars. It was *food* Princess needed, and she could think of nothing but the Tastee Tidbits that would be waiting in her own kitchen. And milk—how she longed for a saucer of sweet, warm milk!

It seemed an endless time before the mean lady and her family had finished breakfast and gone back into the house. The morning sun was already high in the sky before Princess dared to show herself on the boardwalk again — and this time she was cautious. Remembering that awful thumping broom, she slithered up the steps one at a time, showing only the top of her head as she peered over the edge at the terrible house.

They were gone, safely gone. There was still a faint sound of voices inside, but the porch was deserted and there wasn't a sign of life anywhere. Creeping silently across the boardwalk, Princess hid briefly in a tuft of long grass, then dashed to the safety of the bushes surrounding the next porch.

And then she went on to the next, and the next. Soon the lingering breakfast smell was far behind her, and she could pick up other scents. Now and then, stopping to sniff at something that seemed familiar, Princess padded hopefully up and down porch steps, perking her ears for the sound of Mary Ellen's voice inside one of the houses.

But there were no voices—only the screaming of seagulls overhead, crying for food and reminding her of her own fierce hunger. Moving almost at a run, Princess felt her nose twitching at the very thought of breakfast in her own kitchen. But she was nearly at the end of the boardwalk now, and her house was nowhere in sight.

Suddenly she stopped, a terrible thought in her head. Could it be that she was going the wrong way? Could it be that her house was at the *other end*? With a faint, discouraged meow, Princess sat down in the middle of the boardwalk, not knowing what to do.

But then, staring vaguely out over the sunny beach, Princess suddenly saw the old familiar jetty that curved out into the bay, just where the houses stopped — the jetty she'd seen a thousand times from her own front porch!

At once Princess was on her feet, dashing wildly from one sandy front yard to another. Suddenly all the houses began to look familiar. There was the one with the window boxes full of bright flowers — and then the one with the twin stone ducks at the edge of the boardwalk — and then — yes! The one with the falling-down stone fireplace in the front yard. How well she remembered the good smells that came out of it on warm evenings! *Her* fireplace — *her* house!

With a glad meow, Princess flew to the front steps — and then she knew for sure. There, just where she always left them, lay Mary Ellen's torn old beachshoes, and beside them the familiar, rusty old bucket she used for catching crabs!

For a moment, flying up the steps and pacing happily over the sun-warmed boards of the porch — *her* porch! — Princess didn't notice that everything wasn't exactly the same. Fondly sniffing at every well-remembered crack in the floor, she heard herself softly purring for the first time in all the days she'd been lost. Home! She was home!

But then, looking about for the creaky old swing

she used to take naps in, Princess discovered that it was gone. The old wooden rockers were missing too, and not a single beach towel hung over the railing, drying in the sun.

Puzzled, she stalked uneasily over the bare boards, hearing no sound but the soft padding of her own feet. Why were there no voices inside, no breakfast dishes clattering, no footsteps? The bright sun was nearly overhead now—surely they ought to be up and about! They'd never been a family for sleeping late, and she couldn't imagine what was keeping them.

And then, all of a sudden, Princess knew where they were. Leaping swiftly to the wide porch railing, she began squinting eagerly up and down the sunlit beach, searching for the familiar brightly flowered umbrella they set up every morning, for familiar brown legs stretched out underneath it. But it wasn't there!

Far along the shore, the children she'd spotted earlier were still playing at the water's edge, and just behind them a lady in a wide hat was plunging a beach umbrella into the sand. But it wasn't a flowered umbrella—it was plain—and the lady in the hat wasn't Mary Ellen's mother!

Where *were* they? Frantically Princess sprang

from the railing and began scratching at the front door. Raising her faint, forlorn meow to an anguished howl, she called and called — but no one answered. There was no sound at all inside, not a hurrying footstep, not a welcoming voice, not even a whisper. Perhaps, if she could just get a look inside...

But as she crouched, wriggled, and prepared to leap to a window ledge, Princess suddenly saw that the windows were nailed shut and that inside the shades were drawn. Beyond them there was nothing but an awful, echoing silence, and Princess suddenly knew that they had gone. Gone for good— leaving her behind as carelessly as Mary Ellen's discarded old shoes!

Well—not carelessly, she supposed. She couldn't imagine that they had stopped loving her, and in her heart she knew that they had searched and called—maybe even waited an extra few days in the hope that she'd turn up again. But in the end, while she was wandering deeper and deeper into strange fields, they must finally have told themselves that their delicate Princess had died of cold or hunger, and that she was gone for good. Poor Mary Ellen! How she must have cried when they packed up the empty cat case and drove away!

For a long time, Princess sat mournfully on the empty porch, wondering whether she would ever see her family again. She couldn't remember a single summer that they hadn't come here, to this very house — but how many days had to pass until another summer came?

It would be a long time, she knew that, and a hard, cold time. Never in all her life had she been allowed outdoors in winter weather, and until the last terrible weeks out in the fields, she had never even known what it was like to be cold and wet. How on earth was she to keep herself warm when winter came?

And what would she eat? When the last of the summer people had gone, there'd be no hope of being taken in — or at least fed — by a kind person, and there wouldn't even be picnic leavings on the beach. There were always mice, of course, but when snow covered the fields, would they still be running about? Would the birds stay here through the winter? Or would they disappear as mysteriously as the ones at home always did?

A horrifying thought suddenly popped into her head as she remembered her awful hunger. Would her family *know* her when they came back? She was already as gaunt and skinny as a common alley cat, she knew that, and her dingy, greying fur was far from the shining white they would remember. Maybe they'd mistake her for an unknown, starving stray and chase her away!

But no! Suddenly Princess was sure they'd know her, no matter how dreadful she looked. They would know her by her glowing amber eyes (at least *they* hadn't changed!), by her perky, tufted ears, and by all the old, familiar tricks she would do the minute she saw them.

She would stand up on her hind legs to be patted, rubbing her whiskers along their fingers, and then she would pull her claws in and grab the hand that patted her, begging for more. She would roll kittenishly over on her back, waving her paws about, telling them she'd like to play with a dangled string. Yes, they would know. She was sure of it.

But right now, with all the long, cold, hungry days she knew lay ahead, her old world of warmth and love seemed far away. Right now all she could think of was food, and after that—if she could find a way to get herself into the house—a nice cozy spot to curl up in. It wasn't going to be easy, keeping herself alive, but she'd done it so far, hadn't she?

With the brisk September breeze ruffling her fur,

reminding her of chilling days to come, Princess dashed down the steps and around the house to the back road.

Then, thinking of nothing but the fearsome hunger that was gnawing at her insides, she was off into the fields in search of a fat mouse.

Minerva

The dry grass was alive with rustlings, and in no time at all Princess had caught herself not only a mouse, but a few spindly grasshoppers as well. The green wings stuck unpleasantly to her whiskers, but the taste was surprisingly sweet, and at least it was something more to eat. Hopping toads were everywhere, too, and Princess was glad to know that food was not hard to find. At least not now. When winter came —

Winter! The very thought made her shudder, and in a moment she was bounding back across the road, eagerly circling her house in search of open windows. But there were none. Wooden shutters were closed firmly over every one of them, and there wasn't so much as a crack anywhere. Even the garage door at the back of the house was bolted firmly shut, and its tiny, cobwebby window as well.

For a long time Princess paced about the sandy yard, staring up at the closed windows, even leaping hopefully to a window ledge now and then. But it was no use. There was no way at all to get herself inside. The first chill of late afternoon was in the air, and Princess felt herself shivering at the thought of another long cold night outdoors.

And then, just as she was settling herself underneath a bush beside the porch steps, she suddenly discovered that she could get in after all. Well—not *in* exactly—but *under!* All around the lower part of the house ran a wall of slatted trelliswork, and as she peered into the holes between the slats, Princess could see bright spots of sun dappling the dark earth inside. It wasn't exactly a cozy place—but at least it would be dry in rainy weather, and a shelter from the chilling winds that blew across the fields at night.

Once again, hoping to discover a missing slat somewhere, Princess began circling the house, inspecting the trelliswork inch by inch. Never, not in all the years she'd lived upstairs in snug comfort, had Princess considered the place worthy of more than a passing sniff—it had always seemed so damp and cold!—but now she was desperate. It would do, she decided, at least until she could find something better.

At first, peeping curiously through the little holes, Princess couldn't see a thing inside. Then, as her eyes grew accustomed to the darkness, she thought she noticed something moving in a corner — something furry, wriggling in a spot of sunlight. More than one thing, it seemed to be — and very tiny. It was — yes, she was sure of it! — a pile of plump little mice!

Lashing her tail in excitement, Princess paced frantically back and forth, trying to find a way in. The awful, gnawing pain in her stomach was gone now, but she knew she'd be wildly hungry again long before morning. Imagine! A whole supply of mice in her very own house! If she could just get to them —

But it wasn't easy. She was halfway around the house before she found a hollow under the trelliswork that was big enough to squeeze through—and even then it was a struggle. Jagged little splinters caught in the tufts of her ears as she pushed her head underneath the bottom board, and she could feel damp, sandy earth clinging to her fur as she dragged the rest of herself inside. But Princess scarcely noticed. She was going to be warm and dry tonight — and oh, what a supper she'd have!

Slowly and silently, Princess moved across the hard-packed earth floor, keeping her eye on the wriggling mass in the corner. At just the right moment she would pounce, and then —

"Me _ ee _ ow!"

Before she knew what was happening, Princess felt a sharp, pointed claw slashing across her nose, and at once she was backed, trembling, into a corner. Clearly this was no mouse house!

Again she felt the sharp claw — this time yanking a tuft of fur from her delicate ear — and with a yowl of pain, Princess began scrabbling at the bottom board of the trelliswork, searching wildly for the place she'd come in. She felt an angry tug on her tail, and as she whirled about in fright, another swat across her torn, tender nose.

"Please!" she wailed. "Please don't scratch me any more! I didn't know anybody lived here! If you'll just show me how to get out again —"

Princess felt her heart thumping as she waited fearfully for another attack — but to her surprise, none came.

"Nothing but a scared housecat, I see," came a sudden calm voice out of the darkness, "but how did I know that?"

"I meant no harm," pleaded Princess. "Please let me out. I've never had to fight before, and I don't know how!"

"I'm not much for fighting myself," came the strange voice. "Waste of time and energy, if you ask me. But a mother can't be too careful, that's what I always say."

A pair of blazing green eyes were suddenly staring at her through the darkness, and Princess cowered against the trelliswork, wondering which way to run.

"What are you doing in my house, may I ask?"

"I was just—passing by," Princess said in a faint, shaky voice, "and — and I thought I saw a pile of mice in the corner, that's all. I thought —"

"*Mice?*" Suddenly Princess found herself face to face with a bony, angry looking Calico cat. "Did I hear you say *mice*? I'll thank you to look again! Pile of mice indeed!"

Timidly, Princess peered over the Calico's shoulder, then took a few careful steps toward the wriggly patch of sunlight in the corner.

"Kittens!" she marvelled. "A whole family of

cuddly kittens! Honestly, if I'd known —"

"Well, you certainly *should* have known," sputtered the Calico. "Imagine mistaking *my* family for nothing more than a silly pile of mice! I've never been so insulted in all my life!"

"They're adorable," murmured Princess, hoping to soothe their furious mother, "every one of them."

"And they all look like *me*," boasted the Calico, looking suddenly proud and pleased, "don't you think?"

"Well, they—" Princess glanced politely from the kittens to their mother and back again. "Well, there *is* a sort of resemblance."

But there wasn't, really. The kittens were plump and fuzzy and cute, but—though she couldn't very well say so — Princess thought their mother just about the ugliest cat she had ever seen. All spots and stripes and patches — and skinny! The poor thing looked as though she hadn't eaten a square meal in *months*.

She had a kind face, though—now that the anger had faded away — and before long Princess felt comfortable enough to sit down and begin licking casually at her rumpled fur.

"Tell me," she said politely, "is this where you

live? I mean, all the time? Surely you belong to somebody — ?"

"I belong to nobody," the Calico announced proudly. "I'm free as the air. I come and go as I please, I do what I like, I set up housekeeping wherever I choose." Feeling entirely safe now with her mild-mannered visitor, she turned and settled herself contentedly into the pile of old rags and newspapers that was apparently her bed. Then she gave her kittens a motherly lick, and gazed dreamily through the trelliswork. "The independent life — that's the life for old Minerva. Nothing like it, my dear, let me tell you. Peace, quiet, not a worry in the world —"

"But how on earth do you manage? I've had such a time of it myself, and I've only been lost a week or two." Princess was amazed. Imagine being satisfied with a grubby old pile of rags for a bed! And never a decent, civilized dish of catfood or even a saucer of milk! "What do you find to eat every day?"

"Oh, field mice, mostly," Minerva said casually, "though now and then I enjoy a bit of seafood. I just stroll along the beach at low tide, and you'd be surprised at all the good things I find. Crabs, mussels, clams — even an occasional fresh fish, if he happens to be a slow mover. Then, of course, there are always garbage cans to poke around in, at least in the summer, and —"

"Garbage cans?" Princess was horrified. "How dreadful!"

"I manage," Minerva said calmly. "Did you ever see a healthier batch of kittens in your life?"

"Never," said Princess. She had, in fact, seen very few kittens *ever*, but she couldn't remember any that were any plumper and cuter than Minerva's. "I don't know how you do it. Certainly no housecat I've ever seen took better care of her family than you do."

"I used to be housecat myself," Minerva said. "Would you believe that? Honestly, nowadays I wonder how I ever put up with it! People forever chasing me off sofas the minute I had myself settled down for a nice snooze, pouncing on me just when I had my eye on a juicy sparrow, tying scratchy ribbons around my neck on holidays — ah, the indignities a housecat has to suffer! But all that was a long time ago. I was just a little bit of a thing then, and—"

"But what happened? Did they leave you?"

"No," Minerva said proudly. "*I* left *them*. They had a perfectly terrible dog — yippy little terrier named Butch — that I simply couldn't stand, and besides that there was a pesky little girl who was forever trying to dress me up in doll clothes and push me down the boardwalk in a carriage — imagine! So one day, I simply up and went. But it wasn't easy getting myself lost."

"Why not?"

"Because" — Minerva couldn't help an amused twitch of her whiskers at the memory — "I was wearing a *bonnet*! And long, trailing skirts! I was days getting rid of the stuff, let me tell you — nearly strangled myself in those silly bonnet strings! And then I just wandered in the fields until summer was over, and when it began getting chilly, I moved in here. Been here ever since."

"And I never knew," marvelled Princess. "I've been living upstairs all summer, and I never knew."

"Well, it's a pleasure having you drop in, even if you did mistake us for — uh — something else. I get lonely sometimes, now that my husband has wandered off again. But then, he always was a shiftless type — no brains and no manners." Minerva twitched her nose scornfully at the memory of her wandering husband, then stared admiringly at Princess. "I can see that *you* have manners. What do they call you?"

"The Princess of Avalon." Licking delicately at her matted fur, Princess tried hard to look worthy of the name. "Pretty, isn't it? My family found it in a book of fairy tales. But of course they call me Princess for short. They only use the whole thing for cat shows."

"Cat shows?" Minerva looked puzzled. "What on earth are cat shows?"

"Well, they get all these cats together — oh, just dozens and dozens of them, all kinds—and then they put them all in this great big room, and—"

"But do they *stay* there?" Minerva couldn't believe her ears. "How do they get them to stay?"

"They're all in cages, naturally, and so—"

"*Cages?*" Minerva looked horrified. "Did you say they put them in cages? *Cats?*"

"Not for long," said Princess. "Only while they're waiting to be shown."

"But what's the point? What do they *do* in those cages?"

"Oh—eat, sleep, look beautiful. And people stroll up and down looking at them."

"And then what?"

"Then they parade them around a ring, one by one, and decide which ones are best."

"What for?"

"Well— just to see — um — well — the very best ones get to take home a ribbon. *I* got one once."

Princess couldn't help swelling with pride. "A blue one, with gold lettering on it."

"I'd rather take home a good piece of fish for my pains," sniffed Minerva, "but then, I suppose it takes all kinds. Some cats like to wear ribbons, I guess."

"Oh, you don't *wear* them," said Princess, wondering why she felt suddenly foolish. "You — uh — hang them on the wall and look at them."

For a long, puzzled moment Minerva was silent, trying hard not to smirk rudely at the thought of a useless ribbon hanging on the wall over a *caged* cat. Really, the things some cats had to put up with! She shook her head pityingly. Then, not wanting to hurt Princess's feelings, she politely changed the subject.

"I suppose you'll be leaving soon?"

To her surprise, Princess began crying softly.

"No," she said. "There's — there's no place to go. They left me, you see, and —"

"They *left* you?" Minerva was stunned. "A prize cat — with a *ribbon*? But how could they? I mean, if you were just a plain old Calico like me, well, that's one thing, but —"

"Oh, they didn't mean to, I know they didn't. But I got lost. Terribly, horribly lost — and oh, I've just been wandering and wandering — and of course they had to go home when the time came, and now—"

"How awful for you." Minerva was all sympathy. "I guess if you're used to nice warm — ugh! — cages, and regular meals and everything, the country life can seem pretty hard."

"Oh, it *is*!" Miserably, Princess looked down at her tangled fur. "Just look at me—all burrs and sand and dirt and snarls! What I wouldn't give for a good brushing! We long-hairs need help, you know. We can't accomplish a whole lot just by licking."

"I'll help," Minerva offered kindly. "Come on over here and I'll do the top of your head where you can't get at it. And if you don't mind a bit of yanking, maybe we can get rid of the worst of those burrs, too." Her mouth was curled into a welcoming smile. "Come on. There's plenty of room. You can cuddle up with the rest of us and help me keep the kittens warm when the snow comes."

When the snow comes! The words sent such a shiver down Princess's spine that she could feel her fur standing on end. Snow! Oh, and wind and rain! The very thought of the winter to come made her long for warmth, and at once she padded gratefully toward Minerva. At least she had a friend!

"Move over a bit there, Sam," commanded

Minerva, "and you, too, Sarah. We've got company!"

Almost at once, nestled comfortably among the kittens, Princess began to feel better. Starting up her rusty purr, she began rhythmically kneading her claws in the soft rags as Minerva went efficiently to work on the top of her tattered head.

Winter Comes

All through the first crisp days of September, bright sun sparkled over the fields, and Princess was surprised to discover that her strange new life wasn't bad at all. It was, as a matter of fact, almost fun!

From the beginning, she was like an aunt to the kittens, taking care of them all by herself whenever Minerva was out prowling the fields for mice and birds, keeping them all in a nice cozy heap until their mother came home to feed them. Sometimes she played with them, pretending annoyance when they pounced on her switching tail, and sometimes she just cuddled them while they snoozed the hours away.

There was plenty of food, too, thanks to Minerva. Princess never did get used to the strange tasting little wild creatures they caught in the fields, but at least she wasn't hungry any more. Minerva never so much as bothered with the frightened, scurrying baby mice that were all Princess had ever managed to catch, and soon taught her to settle for nothing but the biggest, fattest, and juiciest.

Sometimes, leaving the kittens asleep, Minerva led Princess all the way down to the water's edge, showing her all sorts of delicacies Princess had never even seen before. She had often strolled the sunny beach herself, back in the old days, but the thought of getting her feet wet had always kept her safely close to the boardwalk. Now, with Minerva scampering ahead of her among the barnacled rocks of low tide, Princess discovered dozens of brand new treats — and some of them were even better than Tastee Tidbits!

There were popped-open clams and mussels, crabs with shells soft enough to crack with a sharp claw, and, once in a while, fresh fish. Minerva taught her how to perch silently beside a rocky pool, watching for a glint of silver in the sunlit water, then swoop a lightning-fast paw down into the pool at the first sign of something moving. She taught her how to reach underneath rocks, groping for wiggly crabs, and whenever the catch was slim, how to make a surprisingly decent meal out of the chewy, salt-tasting seaweed that was freshly washed up on the beach every day.

A few garbage cans still stood behind the garages on the back road, too, and Minerva inspected them every day. Somehow Princess couldn't bring herself to rummage about in the nasty things herself, but she had to admit that once in a while Minerva really turned up something worthwhile, like a delicious scrap of cooked meat, or a chicken bone with lots left on it.

It wasn't a way of life Princess would have chosen, but it wasn't as bad as she had expected, either. Minerva was right — there *was* a lot to be said for independence. For one thing, it was nice to eat whenever she happened to be hungry, instead of having to wait for a proper mealtime. It was nice to stroll about whenever and wherever she chose, without having to wait for somebody to open a door. And what a good feeling it was to sharpen her claws on a real tree trunk instead of that silly little scratching post that always fell over the minute she jumped on it. No, it wasn't a bad life at all—at least so far.

Sometimes, though, on nights when the autumn wind blew through the trelliswork, she couldn't help thinking wistfully about her snugly carpeted city home, her wicker cat bed with a real mattress in it, daily meals served to her in a dish—and oh, how she longed for the daily brushing someone always gave her! Though Minerva was terribly nice about helping her with the hard parts, like the top of her head and the spot just under her chin where licking was impossible, a small pink cat tongue just wasn't as good as a sturdy brush, and she knew she wasn't going to look like much when her family came back. Still, she thought gratefully, she was *alive* — and that was something.

It was not until the middle of October, when it suddenly began to rain—and rain—and *rain*—that she felt the first tremors of fear.

"How on earth are we going to find food *now*?" she asked bleakly, staring through the trelliswork at the whipping, lashing rain. "We'll get ourselves soaked!"

"Best time," Minerva said calmly. "The more rain

the better. The mice get flooded out, you see, and then they're all over the fields. You don't even have to look for them."

"But I'm terribly susceptible to colds. The vet said I should be kept indoors during rainy weather. He said — "

"What's a — vet?"

"Well, he's a person who takes care of animals when they're sick. He pokes pills down their throats and sticks them with needles, and then they feel better."

"Oh," said Minerva, looking blank, "I see." But of course she didn't. She couldn't imagine how sticking a needle into a cat would make it feel better, but if Princess said so, then it must be true. She was a *show* cat, after all, and although Minerva often felt contemptuous of the cramped, stuffy life Princess described to her, she couldn't help feeling a bit envious now and then. It must be terribly nice to be admired all the time, she often thought wistfully. Though she had always been entirely pleased with her own appearance (thought herself remarkably pretty, in fact), she could stroll the whole length of the boardwalk, in broad daylight, without anyone so much as noticing her.

Oh well, that was one of a very few drawbacks to

the independent life. At least she didn't get colds (whatever they were) and have to be stuck with a needle. She looked pityingly at Princess, all huddled in a ball under an ancient pair of discarded oars, trying to keep herself warm. Poor thing!

"What really worries me," Princess was saying plaintively, "is that sooner or later it's going to turn to *snow*. And then what will we do?"

"Snow is warm," Minerva said mysteriously. "You just wait and see."

It was, too. To Princess's astonishment, when snow began piling up against the trelliswork, it blocked the cold north wind, and they were far cozier than they had been through the damp, chilly months of early fall. And on the south side of the house, the first wet, thick snows of winter always melted quickly enough so that they could get out for food.

But pickings grew slimmer and slimmer as the weather grew colder. Down on the beach — when they could get there at all — snow covered the piles of seaweed washed up by the waves, and sometimes it was days before the stuff thawed out enough for them to crunch into it. There were no crabs or clams now, either, and of course the dark, wind-whipped water of the bay was far too icy for fishing.

Even mice, buried deep in the frozen fields, were hard to come by, though happily there were quite a few who had either forgotten to dig holes, or had chosen to live in vacant garages. They were forever scurrying in and out underneath the cracks below the doors, and a little patient watching and waiting always brought them a decent catch. A few birds lingered, too, and Minerva was a whiz at spotting chipmunks scampering over the snow, even pouncing on an occasional unwary squirrel.

And so they survived, but it wasn't easy. The kittens were growing far too old now for mother's milk alone, and Minerva was finding it harder and harder to bag enough game for all of them. But she managed somehow, and — to her own astonishment — Princess was a deft and willing helper. Oddly, she didn't catch a single cold, and though she was soon as gaunt and skinny as Minerva, she had never felt more fit in her life.

There were times, though — dreadful, bone-chilling, starving times — that Princess honestly thought might mean the end of them all. Sudden violent snowstorms sometimes trapped them inside — once for a whole long day and a night — and there was no way to get food at all. They kept themselves alive by chewing on the brown, withered weeds sticking up through the snow outside, and lapping at whatever melted snow trickled inside their home. Nothing more!

Sometimes, trying not to hear the pitiful mewing of the hungry kittens, Princess would curl up in a corner, close her eyes, and dream of home. It was the time of year, she remembered, when particularly good smells came out of the kitchen, and when scraps of delicious chopped up turkey meat suddenly began to appear in her dish. It was the time of year when everybody gave everybody else presents, and her old, chewed-up catnip mice were thrown out in favour of brand new, fresh-smelling ones.

And for her special amusement, they always brought a live pine tree into the house, and hung pretty toys on it. For some reason, they tried to keep her from batting at them—but what else could they be for? Their stern "nos," she decided, were just part of a special game, and she found it great fun to sneak up to the tree when no one was in sight, and knock as many shining balls to the floor as she could. They always pretended anger when they found broken ones, but sooner or later someone always patted her and called her "cute," and then— as soon as they were all gone—she'd play the game again.

But there were no games now (except for an occasional foolish romp with the kittens), and the very thought of a pine tree was hateful. Minerva had shown her, one day when their hunger was truly awful, how to rip bits of bark from the trunk and then — ugh! — make a meal out of them. She never could manage to swallow much of the stuff (though it was surprisingly sweet-tasting) without choking on the splinters, but she had to admit that it soothed those dreadful, gnawing hunger pains, at least for a while. There was always just plain water to fill up on, too, and though Princess had never much bothered about it back in the days when warm milk had been served at least twice a day, she was amazed to discover that a good long drink of water could get her through a whole night without her stomach growling.

And then — just when an unexpected thaw fooled them into thinking spring was finally coming — they were struck by the mightiest blizzard that even Minerva had ever seen. For two long days the swirling, stinging snow trapped them under the house, and in all that time they ate nothing — *nothing*! The growing kittens grew wobbly on their little legs, and instead of playing, they huddled forlornly together in their pile of rags, mewing and mewing.

"It's no use," Minerva suddenly said on the afternoon of the second day. "I'm going to have to go out." She was pacing restlessly from one corner to another, squinting grimly out into the blowing snow, looking for a place where the wind had blown a clearing. "There's sure to be a fallen bird somewhere, or maybe a lost rabbit. Even a bit of pine bark would keep us alive — if I could just get myself to the woods."

"But you can't!" Princess was thunderstruck. "It's deep! You'll never be able to make a path for yourself, and with the wind blowing every which way, you're sure to get lost."

"Me?" Minerva stopped her pacing and glared at Princess. "Me — lost? Don't be silly. I have never been lost in my entire life! And I've been out in blizzards before, too. You needn't worry about *me!*"

"But the wind —"

"Never mind the wind. Wind is helpful, didn't you know that? It blows the snow into drifts, and then you can walk on the bare spots. Sometimes you can even find some grass to chew on, and if you're really lucky, a frozen mouse or two. And remember, I'm a mother. I've got my family to think about."

"Yes," Princess finally agreed, looking sorrowfully at the little pile of hungry kittens, "I guess you'll have to try. And in the meantime, maybe I can dig a few holes close by. I just might be able to turn up something. But please — don't go too far. Don't get lost."

Once again Minerva turned to glare at Princess.

"I have never," she sniffed, "been lost in my entire life."

And then, as Princess watched fearfully, Minerva wriggled swiftly out under the icy trelliswork, and was gone.

The Blizzard

For a long way, there was a beautifully windswept path, with snow no higher than the tops of her legs, and despite the whirling flakes that stung her eyes, Minerva was able to go a considerable distance toward the woods. She couldn't see the trees yet, but she was dead certain she was headed in the right direction. If she just didn't run into any impassable drifts along the way, she'd be there in a jiffy.

Wonder of wonders, she actually stumbled across a tiny, frozen mouse, and for a moment she thought of carrying it swiftly back to the babies. But no — it was so small! Sensibly she decided to eat it herself, for strength, and then go on into the woods to see if she could find something big enough to feed them all.

A rabbit, she thought, was her best bet, and from long experience she knew that winter was the best time for rabbit hunting. If she just had strength enough to reach the woods, she knew she'd be able to catch one without much of a struggle. She had long since discovered that rabbits — though fast — are not at all smart. Despite the fact that brown fur stands out clear and sharp against white snow, the foolish creatures didn't seem to know this and so they generally froze motionless, hoping not to be seen. And then, of course, it was a simple matter to pounce.

Crunching fiercely into the skinny, hard little mouse she'd found, Minerva made short work of the one and only meal she'd had in a day and a half, and then looked eagerly about for more mice. But there were none. Snow was piling up all around her, and she could feel the flakes clinging to her fur and freezing into tiny icicles. No point in searching further, not now. Vaguely she remembered another snowstorm, another year, when the clinging snow had frozen her so stiff she could hardly move, and she knew at once that she'd have to thaw herself out a bit before she could move quickly enough to catch even a stupid rabbit.

Ghostly grey shadows loomed through the whiteness, and Minerva thought they must surely be the pine trees. Battling the wind, she inched her way forward through the driving flakes, longing for shelter. Though the woods would be piled high with snow too, she knew there would be low-hanging branches, protecting the ground and making little covered nooks of nearly bare earth. She could hollow herself a little nest, with walls of snow all around to keep her out of the whipping wind. There might even be a fallen pinecone or two to chew on, and then — if darkness didn't come too soon — she could venture out to scout for rabbits.

But it was growing dark now, and the whiteness all around her was beginning to turn grey. There wasn't so much as a bush in sight, and Minerva knew she'd have to get herself all the way into the woods before she found shelter. Thoughts of her wobbly-legged, mewing kittens drove her on, and though the windswept path had nearly disappeared, somehow she managed to pounce her way through snow that was nearly over her head by now.

The woods! At last! At the very edge, Minerva

stopped for a moment, finding her legs suddenly weak, and then — thinking she'd spotted a fallen bird a few feet away — wearily pounced herself toward it over the deepening snow. But it wasn't a bird! It was nothing but a feathery, broken-off branch from a pine tree, and there wasn't even a pinecone on it to chew!

Staggering now, Minerva fought her way through the biting wind, remembering Princess and the babies, remembering that they were even hungrier than she. How long, she wondered bleakly, could they go on without food? Would a gentle, city cat like Princess — earnest as she was about learning all her lessons — actually be strong enough to brave a blizzard? She didn't know, and in a moment, knocked clean off her feet by a sudden icy blast of wind, she found herself thinking of nothing at all but a warm, dry place for herself.

And then, suddenly she spotted something — a small, dark, moving something — just over the rise of the drift she was floundering through. It seemed to be struggling through the deepening snow, pounce by pounce, just as she was, and for a moment she wondered whether it might be another starving cat, out looking for food. It was hard to see through the whirling, stinging flakes, and it was a long, weary time before she was able to inch herself close enough to see what the creature might be.

All at once her awful, aching exhaustion was gone, and Minerva felt her heart thumping in excitement as she brought herself to a shaking, quivering halt — and saw that it was a rabbit! A not very bright, lost rabbit, wondering frantically what had become of its nice warm hole! With telling scents all driven away by the wind, the silly creature didn't know she was anywhere about, and Minerva watched intently as it began munching on a clump of dried grasses sticking up through the snow.

Slowly, cautiously, she worked her way out of the snowdrift, out to a nearly bare, windswept spot. And then, lowering herself to her belly, she began to stalk. It was important, now, not to hurry, no matter how hungry she was. Though the snow muffled any sound she might otherwise have made, she knew that the rabbit would spot any sudden motion out of the corner of its eye, and would be gone in a bound. And so she took her time, moving slowly and silently, keeping her tail stretched out behind her, absolutely still. The rabbit was crouched down, blind to everything but the grass it was chewing, not even faintly aware of danger.

When the distance between them was exactly right, Minerva gathered her strength, wriggled from side to side for momentum — and pounced. In a flash she had sunk her teeth fiercely into the rabbit's neck; red blood was spurting out onto the white snow, and a resounding crack told her that the creature's neck was broken. Feebly it kicked its feet, thrashing about under Minerva's body, and then — after one faint, anguished cry — it was still.

There! She had done it! She had caught herself a full-grown rabbit (a rather scrawny one, she noted ruefully, but certainly large enough to tide them all over for a day or two) and she couldn't help feeling very pleased with herself. For a moment, breathing heavily, she sat back to rest — not even troubling to wash her bent, bloody whiskers — and then she seized the rabbit by a hind leg and began dragging it through the snow, toward home.

At the edge of the field, she stopped. It was much darker now, and all at once Minerva knew that she would have to wait for morning. She, who had never been lost in her entire life, had better sense than to go stumbling off into a blinding blizzard in the dark of night, and so she turned about and headed toward the woods, dragging her catch behind her.

She found a fine, low-hanging branch to crawl under, and though it was difficult to haul the heavy rabbit in along with her, she was determined not to lose it. Besides, she'd need a bit of nourishment herself if she was to have enough strength for tomorrow's journey. In a moment she was tearing hungrily at the rabbit's skinny leg.

And then, just as she was beginning to wash up, and was thinking about licking the ice from between her toes, there was a mighty crack overhead — and a slim branch, heavy with snow, suddenly broke from the tree and crashed down upon her. Startled by the sound, Minerva didn't know at first what had happened. But then, in the merest instant, there was another, smaller crack, and a searing, white-hot pain suddenly shot wildly up her left hind leg.

A kind of veil, all flashing and sparkling, fell over her eyes, and she heard herself wailing. But her voice seemed to come from far away, as though it belonged to some other creature, and then it faded and disappeared. Suddenly Minerva felt herself drifting soundlessly on an icy sea of pain, into a cold, silent blackness.

In a moment there was no sound anywhere but the angry howling of wind through the pines. Soon the woods grew dark.

A Homecoming

The kittens seemed alarmingly still in their rumpled bed, and though she licked and licked at them, Princess couldn't seem to rouse them from their long, feeble sleep. She curved her warm, furry body close around them, but the poor little things shivered against her, mewing softly, nosing hopelessly into her fur in search of milk. The unending rumble in her own belly told her plainly that she could wait no longer for Minerva, and when morning came she left the kittens and began searching for an opening.

More snow than she had ever seen was piled against the trelliswork, but the furious wind had died down, and no more flakes were falling. Squinting upward through the holes, she could see that the sky was still grey, but there was a brightness about it that told her the storm was over. She didn't have the slightest idea how to go about finding food in all that frozen whiteness, but there wasn't a sign of Minerva, and she knew she'd have to try.

But where? How? Should she dig a hole at the garage door, in the hope that the few remaining mice might come scurrying out? Should she struggle out to the fields in search of winter berries? There'd be no way to carry them back to the babies, of course, but at least she could get up a little strength herself, and then go off on a search for a fallen bird. She remembered flocks of scrawny grey sparrows living in the old dead trees around the swamp, and thought some of the weaker ones might have blown to the ground in last night's furious wind. But how, in all that piled up snow, could she get herself to any of those places? And back?

Sensibly, remembering that Minerva had never been lost in her entire life — and would surely be back soon — she decided to start by digging a few holes around the house, just to see what might be lying around under the snow. Frozen mice, perhaps, and she could peel them down to their inner-most warm organs for the kittens. Or maybe just some grasses with seeds on them. Bits of bark from the scraggly bushes that grew around the house, or (but she didn't really thing she'd be so lucky) the carcass of a frozen squirrel.

With the faint, forlorn mewing of the kittens still in her ears, Princess burrowed her way out from under the trelliswork, and began pouncing her way through the drifts.

On the morning of the very next day, a pale sun broke through the greyness of the sky, and before Princess knew it, the snow close to the house was melting, running in rivulets under the house, giving them all plenty of water to drink. The huge dead bird she had unexpectedly found on the front porch had restored the kittens almost to their usual play-fulness, and although there was nothing left now but a pile of stiff, sticky feathers and bones, at least they'd all be alive and well when Minerva came home.

But where *was* she? Had she, after all, got herself lost for the first time in her entire life? Had she frozen to death out there in that wicked storm? Had a hunter mistakenly shot at her? Or had she simply not yet caught anything worth bringing home?

Restlessly, Princess paced and paced, knowing that soon she'd have to go out again into that awful, icy whiteness, knowing that the dead bird was enough for only a day or two.

Though she'd never been a mother herself, something inside her made her want to take care of Minerva's kittens, but it was a hard thing to do all by herself, without her family to help her. Once, she remembered, Mary Ellen had brought a box of tiny kittens home from the grocery store where they'd been born (they'd been returned the very next day) and though Princess hadn't paid much attention to them herself, Mary Ellen's mother and father had actually sat down and fed them milk through medicine droppers. What she wouldn't give, right now, for human help!

A faint, faraway cry suddenly floated to her over the snow, and in a flash Princess was bounding from one opening to another, trying to decide exactly which direction it came from. Minerva! It must be Minerva! Slipping out under the trelliswork, she leaped to the top of a crusted drift, and began squinting out over the frozen whiteness.

There! Yes, just over there on the rise of a snow-covered dune, something was moving—but slowly, oh so slowly! And it didn't walk like a cat at all. Whatever the creature was, it seemed all lopsided and dragging, and it kept slipping and falling on the crusted snow. For a moment, Princess thought it must be a wounded rabbit, and—though she longed to see Minerva again—she felt her heart pounding in excitement. She had never quite got the hang of pouncing on grown rabbits (they were so *fast*, and they kicked so!) but once in a while she'd been able to catch a baby one, or one that had been injured. This one looked possible.

Twitching her nose hungrily at the thought of fresh meat, she eased her way to the bottom of the drift and began to stalk. Slowly, cautiously, one foot at a time, just as Minerva had taught her. Her tail stood straight out behind her, barely moving, and she knew that the whiteness of her fur against the snow was in her favour. She'd have that lame old rabbit in no time — and oh, how proud Minerva would be when she came home and found a tasty meal waiting for her!

But then the creature made a noise — and it wasn't the shrill squeak of a rabbit! It was, very plainly, a loud, triumphant "Meow!" Minerva had come home!

Eagerly, wondering what on earth was taking her so long, Princess scampered over the snow to meet her.

"I'm hurt," Minerva told her in a faint, exhausted voice. "Something fell on me, and my left hind leg has gone all funny. It doesn't seem to work at all, and let me tell you, I've had quite a time hauling this rabbit home." She was panting, her tongue lolling wearily out of her mouth, and Princess could see streaked blood all over her leg. But—incredibly—she was dragging a full-grown rabbit after her! "I could use some help getting it inside."

"Then you didn't get lost after all," Princess marvelled. "You did find your way home!"

Tired as she was, Minerva pulled her broken body upright and fixed Princess with an angry glare.

"I have never been lost in my entire life. Any cat with half a brain knows enough to wait for daylight, and that is exactly what I did. Now, if you'll just help me get this creature inside, I've got my babies to tend to."

And in a moment, while Minerva dragged herself slowly over the snow, Princess had pulled the rabbit to the house and was fiercely yanking it under the trelliswork. The kittens were tearing at it before she had it more than halfway in, and Princess turned to see how Minerva was faring.

Poor thing! Clearly she was in terrible pain, and her breath came in short, wheezy gasps. By the time she'd dragged herself inside, she was too exhausted even to make the short distance to the pile of rags, but simply flopped to the frozen earth just inside the opening. She was very still, and her eyes were closed.

When the meal was over, a few of the kittens romped to their mother, nosing into her icy fur, pouncing playfully on her faintly lashing tail. Minerva moved a front paw just enough to bat them angrily away, and once, when one of the kittens bumped suddenly into her injured leg, she actually hissed at it. And then she closed her eyes again, breathed deeply, and seemed to sleep.

For many days she lay just where she was, painfully dragging herself to her feet now and then just long enough to nibble at whatever food Princess managed to bring home, or lap feebly at the water running under the trelliswork. Sometimes, watching Minerva's bony sides heaving fitfully as she slept, Princess found herself wondering whether she was ever going to get up again for good — or whether this was to be the end of poor Minerva!

But then, on the very first day the sun shone in a truly blue sky, Minerva suddenly limped all the way to the pile of rags in the corner, licked at a kitten or two, and sank contentedly in among them.

"I am," she announced calmly, "perfectly fine now. Is there still a bit of sparrow left?"

Mary Ellen

Every day now, the sky was beautifully blue and promising, and as soon as the worst of the snow had melted, Minerva decided to teach the kittens how to hunt for themselves. Though she walked in a funny, twisted way now, the bad leg didn't seem to be any more than a silly nuisance to her, and before long she was lolloping about in the fields almost as swiftly as Princess and the kittens.

When the spring thaw came and the fields began showing a delicate, feathery green, the biggest, sturdiest of the kittens bravely left home to seek his own fortune. One by one the others followed, and by the time the first spring birdsong floated over the dunes, they were all gone.

They missed them dreadfully at first, but "that is the way of life," Minerva kept saying sensibly and soon they were glad, both of them, that they had only themselves to think about. They had taught the kittens well and didn't worry. Any children of Minerva's, Princess often thought, would be strong and resourceful and wise. They would be all right.

And now it was Minerva's turn to be fearful. The sun was warmer every day, and of course every warm day brought them closer to summer. Princess's family would be back, they would take her upstairs where she belonged, and then — well, chances were they'd soon spot raggedy old Minerva and chase her out from under the house. Though she'd never been bothered by summer people before (they'd scarcely noticed her quiet comings and goings), she hadn't had a funny, twisty limp before, nor an ugly, jagged scar on her leg. For some reason people always seemed horrified at any sort of ugliness, and though she felt certain that the rest of her was still as pretty as ever, Minerva shrank at the thought that anyone — especially Mary Ellen — might be frightened of her.

"But she *wouldn't* be," Princess kept telling her over and over again. "Mary Ellen isn't like that at all. She wouldn't hurt a living thing, I know she wouldn't. Once she even took a sick little baby bird into the house and kept it in a box, and even dug up worms to feed to it. Ugly little thing it was, too, and she wouldn't let *me* anywhere near it. And then, when it was all well, she took it outside and let it fly away."

"That's not what *I'd* have done with it," sniffed Minerva, "but it's nice to know just the same that your Mary Ellen has a kind heart. Maybe she won't bother me."

"Maybe she'll take *you* upstairs too," suggested Princess, "and let you live with us. She loves cats."

"Not me," Minerva said sorrowfully. "Nobody who owns a valuable show cat would want a gimpy, scratched-up old Calico like me — not even as a guest."

"Wait and see," said Princess, "just you wait and see."

But as she glanced at Minerva's ugly white scar, and then all up and down her skinny, patchy body, she wasn't quite sure either.

"Wait and see," she told herself uncertainly, "just wait and see."

And it wasn't long. A day came when a car crunched suddenly into the stony driveway, footsteps pounded up to the back porch, and then there were all sorts of noises overhead — the creaking of shutters being flung open, dishes clattering in the kitchen, excited voices echoing through the long deserted rooms.

"Are you sure it's not strangers?" Minerva worried. "Are you sure it's the very same family you lived with? Because if it isn't, we might just have to pick up and move. You never know. Strangers just might throw things at us, or —"

"*My* family would never throw things," Princess said firmly, "and it couldn't be anybody else. They *always* come — and before you know it, they'll all be out looking for me. I'm sure they will."

But she wasn't, quite. Maybe they had got themselves another cat by now — a nice, neat, clean one — and maybe they'd forgotten all about their poor lost Princess. Or maybe they wouldn't know her, and little Mary Ellen would be frightened to see such a matted, dingy old creature creeping out from under the house. And could she really expect them to take to poor, scarred-up Minerva with her funny walk and her crazy, patchy coat?

It was a long time before Princess could bring herself to slip out from under the house and around to the front steps, with Minerva — too curious to be scared — padding softly behind her. The old familiar squeak of the screen door told her that someone was coming out, and in a moment small, bare feet were pounding across the porch. And then there was the sound of a ball bouncing down the steps. Mary Ellen, for sure!

Or — and suddenly Princess found herself huddling against the trelliswork, hiding — might it be some other child after all? It seemed a long time before footsteps followed the bouncing ball down the steps, and as she stared out into the sunshine, studying the small figure, Princess was amazed to find that she wasn't at all certain. The child seemed so much bigger than she remembered! Her hair was fixed in a different way, and the short, plump little legs Princess used to rub up against were so much longer and slimmer! Could it really be?

Dodging under a bush, Princess stared and stared. It just might *not* be Mary Ellen — and who knew what terrible thing a strange child might do to her? She couldn't help remembering that awful lady from last summer, the one who had threatened her with a broom — and the shrieking little boy who had chased her off the porch. She had to be sure. Slowly she moved forward, pushing her nose through the leaves for a better look.

The faint rustling sound she made startled the

child, and at once she was down on her knees, peering under the bush. And then, suddenly, she sprang to her feet and backed hastily away.

"Mom! Come quick! There's a cat here — and it might be — it might be Princess! Come quick, Mom! Come see!"

"Oh no, no, no, dear." A lady swung out through the door and leaned over the railing. "It couldn't be. Our Princess couldn't possibly have survived a whole winter all by herself, poor thing. That's a *wild* cat if I ever saw one. Just see what a skinny, bedraggled old thing it is, and how it's all huddled up against the house. It's afraid of you, Mary Ellen, and goodness knows what it might do if you get too close. Now you just come away from that dreadful creature, and I'll shoo it away, and —"

"But the eyes, Mom, the eyes! Those beautiful yellowy eyes — and look! It's got tufty ears too, and curly whiskers — I'll just *bet* that's Princess!"

Slowly, cautiously, Mary Ellen sank to her knees at the foot of the steps, holding out a timid hand.

"Princess? Is it you?"

"No!" her mother said firmly. "You can see that she doesn't know you, Mary Ellen. That is *not* our cat. Just see how she's behaving — all scared and trembly. Our Princess wouldn't —"

"Maybe she just feels strange. I mean, it's been a whole year and everything, and — gee, she *is* scared, isn't she?"

To her own astonishment, Princess suddenly found herself backing away, hissing fiercely. It was something that Minerva had taught her, and by now it was second nature.

"Cats like us can't be too careful," Minerva had warned over and over again, "and if there's the slightest danger, it's best to look mean and keep your distance. A good loud hiss scares them silly, and then you can make a fast getaway if you have to."

And so — after all these months of longing for the sight of her family — here she was greeting them with a hiss and a glare! She simply couldn't help it. Though she knew, now, that it was truly her family, they were acting so skittery and scared — well, they just might decide she was not their Princess after all. And then what? Would they chase her away forever?

Mary Ellen's mother had come down the steps and was fearfully yanking the child away from her.

"See what a dingy grey it is, Mary Ellen, not at all like our beautiful Princess. And look how it's lashing its tail. It doesn't know us, that's for sure, and it's scared to pieces. Now you just come away from that cat before it scratches you!"

And then, all at once, Princess knew just what to do. With a timid, plaintive meow, she moved slowly out from under the bush, toward Mary Ellen's outstretched hand. And then, oh so gently, she rubbed her whiskers along the child's fingers, purring madly. In a moment, Mary Ellen was patting her, smiling up at her mother.

"You see? It *is* Princess! She knows me! And just watch this!"

Mary Ellen rose to her feet, holding her hand just above Princess's head, and at once — just as she used to do all those long, long months ago — Princess stood up on her hind legs, nudging into the hand for another pat, purring and purring.

"It's a miracle!" Mary Ellen's mother bent over to stare into Princess's half-closed amber eyes. "It's an absolute miracle, that's what it is. I can't imagine how she survived the winter, out here by the seashore, all by herself! I can't imagine —"

"But she's not all by herself, Mom. Look! She's got a friend!"

Too curious to hold back another minute, Minerva was poking her head bravely around the side of the house, and in a moment Mary Ellen was bounding toward her.

"Here, puss! Here, puss!"

Bushing up her tail, Minerva began hastily backing away, hissing. Though she'd often told Princess she wouldn't mind a taste of the housecat life again, just for the change, suddenly she knew that they wouldn't like her. They would find her ugly, and then they would chase her away. No! Not if she could make a quick getaway first!

Slowly, trying not to scare anybody, Minerva began backing around the house, growling a low growl, just to keep them at a safe distance. And then, to her astonishment, Princess began meowing pitifully, following after her, calling her back.

"Wait, Princess, wait!" Mary Ellen was running after the two of them. "We won't hurt your friend! She's kind of cute, that's what I think! All those crazy colours all over — kind of like a patchwork quilt. We'll call her — Patches. Here, Patches! Come with Princess! Come on, now. Just stop that silly growling, and I'll get you both some milk."

"Mary Ellen, you come back here this instant! We'll take Princess inside, of course we will, but that other one is wild—maybe even dangerous. Just look at that dreadful scar on its leg! Probably from fighting—and oh, just see what a skinny old bag of bones it is! Probably hasn't eaten in a month, poor thing. But it's got a mean look, Mary Ellen, and I really don't think we should —"

But Mary Ellen was already flying up the steps, into the kitchen for a saucer of milk. In the merest moment,-slopping it over the edges in her haste, she had set the saucer at the foot of the steps.

Milk! Real milk! Princess had almost forgotten the sweet smell of it, and her nose twitched hungrily as she leaped eagerly toward it and began at once to lap it up. Behind her — keeping a wary eye on Mary Ellen's mother — Minerva appeared to be stalking it, as though it were a strange, wild creature, creeping up on it. Then — sensing no hostility whatever — she sidled up beside Princess and began daintily licking a bit from the edges. Then, as she tasted, she began ecstatically opening and closing her claws, purring with pleasure. In no time at all the saucer was empty, and the two cats were frantically bumping heads as their tongues raced around the edges, licking up every drop.

"Just see how hungry they are, Mom! Poor things! And look — this one is going to be friendly. She's not running away or anything. See? All she needs is some good food and a nice home, and she'll be the best old housecat you ever saw. Come on Patches. Come on over here and let me pat you."

But Minerva wasn't ready to be *that* friendly. Goodness, she hadn't been touched by a human hand since she'd been a tiny kitten! It wasn't a thing she could do again without thinking about it for a while.

Backing away again, just a wee bit this time—and without growling or hissing — she settled herself snugly against the trelliswork and began licking drops of milk from her paws, vigorously washing her face. She might be what they called "wild," but she had manners! And whatever happened now, she thought, the memory of that delicious treat would be with her forever. There *was* something to be said for the sheltered life after all, so long as no one came *too* close. Timidly, batting down a bent, damp whisker, Minerva squinted up at Mary Ellen.

"Hasn't she got a nice face, Mom? Don't you think she has? And all those pretty colours all over! You know what? A real Calico is unusual, that's what I've heard. And look at those cute white feet—all four of them alike, as though she's wearing two pairs of little white socks—and just as sparkly clean as anything. She's pretty, Mom! Don't you think she's pretty?"

Pretty! And unusual! Minerva couldn't believe her ears. She was being admired — actually! She, Minerva, who had been so long unnoticed by human beings! She wasn't crazy about the unlovely name, "Patches," but of course they had no way of knowing her real one, and it would do. Yes, any name at all would do if it meant saucers of milk — and a little well-deserved admiration now and then! And maybe, if she could learn a thing or two from Princess about being a proper housecat, maybe she could finally get a crack at those Tastee Tidbits Princess was forever telling her about.

Yes, she might just have another try at the house-cat life. For a while, at least.

End of Summer

It was a glorious, golden summer for both of
them, and as they lazed their days away, napping on
the porch railings and recalling old times, they
found it hard to remember the snow and the wind
and the chilling autumn rain. They grew plump on
the most delicious food Minerva had ever tasted,
and couldn't truly believe they had once been near
starvation. Both of them were brushed and combed
and fussed over (Princess even had a bath), and in
no time at all they were as respectable a pair of
housecats as any that strolled the boardwalk in the
lazy, dusky evenings.

As soon as she was her own magnificently fluffy white self again, Princess was given a brand new blue collar with little silver beads on it, and though Mary Ellen had tried to get Minerva to wear one too, that was going *too* far, and Minerva had clawed it off in a jiffy. It gave her the unpleasant feeling of *belonging* to somebody, a thing she would never do. She would live here, yes — but only because she herself felt like it, and not because anyone said she ought to.

On a long rainy afternoon in late summer, Princess began telling Minerva about the city. The two were snugly curled on the back of the sofa, looking out the window at the rain-spotted bay, feeling glad not to be out roaming the fields or the dunes in search of food.

"It's a cozy way of life," purred Princess, licking a last delicious drop of milk from her whiskers. "You don't ever have to go out in weather like this. In fact, you don't go out at all in the wintertime."

"Not at *all?*" Minerva was startled. "You mean not ever?"

"Oh, now and then they take you for a little walk on a leash," Princess explained, "just for an airing. But with all the cars and the trucks and the buses—

not to speak of dogs — well, it's just not safe. The only time I'm allowed to roam about all by myself is when we're here in the summertime. There aren't so many cars to worry about, you see, and—"

"You mean," Minerva said incredulously, "you go through an entire winter without so much as an occasional mouse hunt? Just for the sport?"

"Oh, I have all sorts of things to play with," Princess boasted, "rubber balls with bells in them, baskets of yarn and string, toy mice—"

"*Toy* mice?" Minerva was astonished. "How on earth do you catch toy mice?"

"Well, you don't exactly — um — catch them," Princess explained lamely. "They're just — there. And when you're feeling frisky, you just kind of bat them around, and chew on them. Some of them have catnip inside."

"Catnip? Is that something you eat?"

"Well, you can. I myself prefer just sniffing it. It has a nice zippy smell to it, and it makes you feel good."

"Oh."

It didn't sound like a whole lot of fun to Minerva, but then, she'd never tried it, so how would she know? At once she cheered herself up with the thought of being warm and dry and well fed all winter. And surely they'd let *her* go out, cars or no cars. Certainly she couldn't imagine putting up with any such fool thing as a leash! Besides, she'd already heard them all worriedly discussing what they called her "wild ways" (she was forever disappearing for days on end) and wondering if she would ever settle down and become a proper housecat.

She would, she thought, in time. Looking sleepily out into the dark, rainy afternoon, she really thought she would.

A day came when they all began bumping trunks and suitcases down the stairs, out the back door, and into the car. Though no one had thought to bring along her old cat case, Princess knew for sure that *this* time she wouldn't be left behind. Nor, she thought, would Minerva, who was coming along so well she had even taken to jumping timidly into a lap now and then when she happened to feel like having her back scratched. Though Minerva continued roaming the fields — even catching an occasional mouse, just for old times' sake — Princess barely stirred from the front porch. The end of summer was no time to get herself lost!

When Mary Ellen called from the kitchen, she was there in a flash—and so, as a matter of fact, was Minerva, who had put off her morning stroll and was waiting impatiently for some sign of food.

"Breakfast is late today," she complained to Princess. "What are they all *doing*? You'd think somebody would remember—"

"They don't feed you when you're going to ride in a car," Princess explained. "They think you might get carsick. Later on, when we get home—"

"Home?" For a moment Minerva looked frightened. "You mean today is the day? I was just on my way down to the beach for a bit of clamming. The tide will be coming in pretty soon, there isn't much time, and—"

"Better not," Princess advised. "They're nearly ready, I think. You don't want to get left behind."

"No," Minerva said nervously, "I guess I don't." But she looked uncertain as she peered out the back door at the car. "I've never ridden in one of those things," she worried, "and it seems kind of a hard thing to face on an empty stomach. And carsick— goodness, I've never been *any* kind of sick in my whole life, though my bad leg did bother me for a time. They don't need to worry about *me*. Do you suppose Mary Ellen is getting some sort of snack out of those boxes?"

In a corner of the kitchen, Mary Ellen was vigorously poking holes in a couple of cardboard cartons, but when she opened the lids, Minerva could see that they were quite empty. At once Mary Ellen began lining them with folded newspapers.

"Okay, Patches," she said cheerfully, "you first. Hold the screen door, Daddy, we're coming!"

Swooping down on the startled Minerva, she picked her up, dangled her over one of the boxes, and then—oh!—began lowering her into it! Kicking wildly with all four feet, Minerva struggled, wriggled, squirmed her way out of Mary Ellen's grip, and leaped through the open doorway. They weren't going to carry *her* out like a box of groceries or a piece of luggage, no indeed! She was not going to get into that box, or any other box, and that was all there was to it!

Oddly—and very much to her own astonishment —neither was Princess. No! Not any more! It was something she remembered, of course — she had been closed up in stuffy cartons and cat cases dozens of times, and never minded a bit—but all that was long ago, far away in another world. Looking out into the wide, welcoming green fields, she suddenly couldn't imagine how she had ever put up with it—that strange, cramped life of cat shows and cages and leashes. Now that she'd had a taste of doing exactly what she pleased, when she pleased, of roaming the fields and the dunes whenever she felt like it, Princess knew with certainty that she was never again going to be anybody's captive, like a silly bird in a cage. No. Not ever again.

Decisively she backed away from Mary Ellen, meowing urgently, trying to tell her that she was positively *not* going to get into that box. Not under any circumstances. She wanted to go home, truly she did, but Mary Ellen had to understand that she was no longer that placid, pampered Princess of Avalon who had once travelled so uncomplainingly in carrying cases. She was different now. Still a housecat, yes—it was her kind of life and she knew it—but a proud, independent housecat, with rights and privileges of her own. And *no more boxes!*

Quickly, not knowing exactly what else to do as Mary Ellen stealthily advanced on her, Princess skittered through the open door, past Mary Ellen's startled father, and—with as much confidence as she could muster—directly into the car.

She'd always had her eye (through the wire mesh of last year's cat case) on the ledge just below the rear window — a delightful spot, she thought, for snoozing in the sun and watching the scenery speeding past. This is where she would ride, she decided, springing lightly upward, just here and no place else.

She thought Minerva would like it too. There was plenty of room to stretch out and be comfortable, and there was even a nice folded blanket to curl up on. Both of them would behave with the utmost dignity, of course, and everybody would know — at last — that she and Minerva were not the sort of cats to be herded into boxes like a couple of helpless kittens. They would choose their own means of travel, thank you. Sternly Princess fixed Mary Ellen's mother, already settled in the front seat, with a proud, decisive glare.

"Well, at least we've got one of them!" Mary Ellen had stuck her head in the window and was looking triumphantly up at Princess. "But I absolutely *couldn't* get her into that box — I guess she's just not used to being cooped up any more — and Patches was even worse. Fought like anything. And then she ran away. I don't know *where* she's got to."

"Probably a mile away by now," sighed her mother. "I don't imagine the poor thing has ever been in a car before, and she's frightened. Maybe she's decided not to come at all."

But Princess knew that was silly. She couldn't remember ever seeing Minerva frightened of *anything*! Chances were she had merely spotted a mouse somewhere, and was having a last pounce or two, just to limber up her muscles for the long ride. Or maybe she just wanted to study the car for a while before she got into it, making sure there was no stuffy box awaiting her.

Squinting out the back window, into the glarey morning sun, Princess thought she caught a glimpse of Minerva's bright calico fur, motionless in a clump of weeds at the end of the driveway. She *wasn't* a mile away, then. She was just taking her time, that was all. How like old, independent Minerva! Princess knew she had every intention of having a fling at the snug city life — she had said so, time and again, over heaping dishes of Tastee Tidbits — but she'd come when she got good and ready, and not before.

Folding her front paws underneath her snowy chest, Princess settled herself comfortably against the sun-warmed glass, and waited. And waited. And waited!

"Where *is* that cat?" Mary Ellen's mother called finally out the front window. "We're all ready to go, and we're getting a late start as it is. We can't wait forever, Mary Ellen. Sooner or later you'll just have to—"

"But we can't *leave* her!" Mary Ellen was frantic. "She's *ours* now, just the way Princess is. Patches! *Here, Patches!*"

There was a sudden bright flash of calico in the clump of weeds, and all at once—while Mary Ellen called forlornly in another direction—Minerva had darted swiftly across the road and hidden herself behind a rock. She would never answer a call, Princess knew that. It was not her way. She would come when she chose to come—or *if* she chose to come. She was not, Princess thought wistfully, "ours," as she herself was. She was not anybody's. How well Princess remembered her proud announcement on the day she had stumbled, all lost and miserable, into Minerva's home for the first time.

"I belong to nobody... I'm free as the air... I come and go as I please, I do what I like, I set up housekeeping wherever I choose...."

Wherever I choose! Suddenly Princess found herself creeping along the ledge, toward the open window, peering worriedly out across the sandy road. Wherever I choose — oh! Was it to be the dunes, then, the frozen fields of winter, the empty, barren beach? Had Minerva forgotten all about Tastee Tidbits, and warm wicker beds with mattresses, and saucers of milk? Was it to be the independent life, forever and always, for Minerva?

For a long moment, sniffing the clean, salty breeze, Princess hovered at the edge of the open window, restlessly lashing her tail, squinting out into the sunshine. How green and open the fields looked, how fresh the pine woods, how inviting the long stretch of sandy beach! And oh, it was the perfect season for popped-open clams, for crabs, for fresh fish. . . .

But the crisp, end-of-summer air hinted of frost to come, stirring a vague memory of ice and snow and howling winds, and suddenly Princess knew for sure that she wanted to go home. Back to her old, snug world of firesides and warm milk and—yes, even cat shows, she thought, just for the sake of being admired now and then. But no more cages, thank you, and no leashes! Not for the new, proud Princess of Avalon who had lived a whole hard year on her own, and had grown nearly as wise as Minerva. Not ever again.

The car engine suddenly started up, and as Mary Ellen crawled dejectedly into the back seat, her face streaked with tears, Princess backed away from the open window, and settled herself—once and for all —on the folded blanket.

With a faint, forlorn cry of farewell, she huddled against the window, watching as Minerva—patchy tail gallantly aloft—slowly disappeared into the tall grass.